The Badge Games

📖 Just Right Reader

Gretchen and her friends, Midge and Fletcher, visited Hatch Park. It was time for The Badge Games!

Kids competed to win badges. They made a pledge to have fun and play nice.

"This time, I will win that kitchen contest," reflected Gretchen.

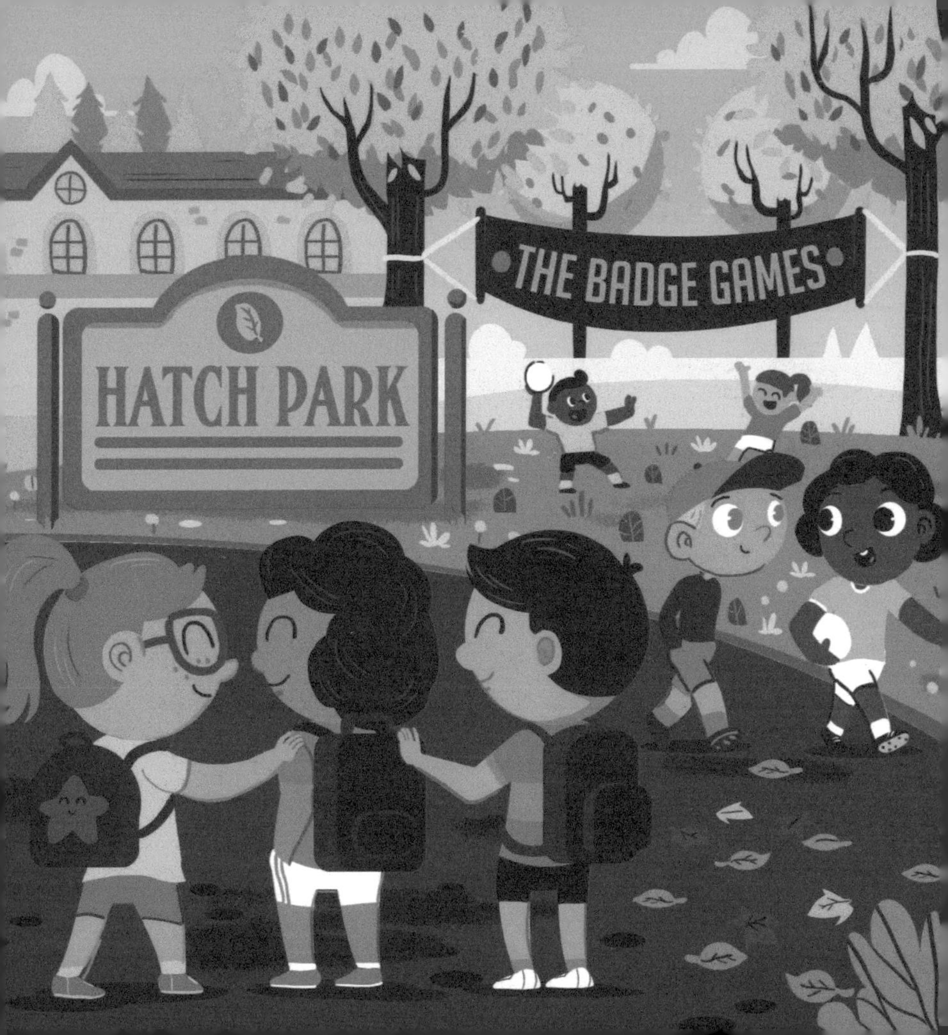
HATCH PARK
THE BADGE GAMES

They watched the judge show them how to stretch. They ran to the edge of the ridge and back.

"Let's go!" said Gretchen, Midge, and Fletcher.

Game one was dodgeball.

"I know how to play," Gretchen said.

But then, Gretchen froze! Her legs just wouldn't budge!

Fletcher won at dodgeball. Fletcher got the dodgeball badge.

The next contest was to sketch something in a kitchen.

Midge's mom is a sketch artist. So Midge watched her mom sketch a lot.

Midge sketched some ketchup. She got the sketching badge.

Next, they played catch on the bridge.

Midge pitched the bag. Fletcher nudged Gretchen out of the way. Gretchen missed the bag. Then Fletcher snatched it!

"We made a pledge to play nice!" said Gretchen.

"I'm sorry!" Fletcher said as he trudged on.

Last was the kitchen contest.

"Now we are making porridge," the judge said.

"I'll be a judge for the porridge!" said Midge.

Gretchen knew how to make porridge.

Fletcher gave her a nudge and said, "I know you can win this, Gretchen!"

Gretchen got milk from the fridge to make the porridge. She added a smidge of salt and a lot of chocolate. It looked like sludge!

Then, the judge wrote "First Place!" on her badge!

"I knew you could do it!" Fletcher said.

Gretchen smiled.

The Badge Games are the best!

Phonics Fun

- Choose 5 words from the list of words in the book.
- Partner 1 reads a word.
- Partner 2 writes it.
- Switch.

 Comprehension

What was the problem in the book? How was it solved?

 High Frequency Words

knew   wrote

 Decodable Words

badge	Midge
bridge	nudge
budge	pitch
catch	pledge
dodgeball	ridge
edge	sketch
Fletcher	sludge
fridge	smidge
Gretchen	snatch
Hatch	stretch
judge	trudge
ketchup	watch
kitchen	